Magic Pony

A Dream Come True

There was a moment's stunned silence, broken by something clumping in Jamie's room. Natty put her head round the door. A real live chestnut pony with one white stocking pawed at the carpet and swished his tail. Natty gasped, eyes as round as pools. It was Ned.

Follow all of Natty and Ned's adventures!
Collect all the fantastic books in the
Magic Pony series:

Magic Pony

A Dream Come True

ELIZABETH LINDSAY

Illustrated by John Eastwood

■ SCHOLASTIC

For Jo, with love and thanks.

Scholastic Children's Books,
Euston House, 24 Eversholt Street,
London, NW1 1DB, UK
a division of Scholastic Ltd
London ~ New York ~ Toronto ~ Sydney ~ Auckland

First published in the UK by Scholastic Ltd, 1997
This edition published in the UK by Scholastic Ltd, 2004

Text copyright © Elizabeth Lindsay, 1997
Illustrations copyright © John Eastwood, 1997

10 digit ISBN 0 439 95961 6
13 digit ISBN 978 0439 95961 2
Fairs edition 10 digit ISBN 0 439 96073 8
Fairs edition 13 digit ISBN 978 0439 96073 1

Printed in the UK by CPI Bookmarque, Croydon, CR0 4TD

10

Contents

Chapter 1
No Time for Pretends

Natty came down the garden path and opened the front gate. In the field on the other side of the lane, Penelope Potter's pony, Pebbles, was dozing in the sun. Yesterday, before Pebbles nearly ate it, Natty had found a four-leaved clover in his field.

Jamie said the clover was incredibly lucky and had tried to buy it, but that's brothers for you. Now it was taped on the wall above her bed, four round leaves and a stalk and, although its greenness was fading, Natty hoped its luck would grow and bring her the pony of her own she had always dreamed of.

There was no sign of Penelope, and Natty wondered if she had time for a secret pretend.

The pretend was to climb the gate, stroke Pebbles's soft nose and imagine he was hers.

"Hurry up, Jamie," Mum shouted from the front door. "We'll miss the bus." She spied Natty by the gate. "I can't think what he's doing."

Natty sighed a big sigh. The pretend would have to wait.

Jamie bounded out of the front door, slamming it behind him, and was at the gate in three leaps.

"Don't hang about," he said, giving Natty a dig. "What you waiting for?"

Jamie was jingling, his pockets full of birthday money, and Mum was taking him to the magic shop in town to spend it. Natty was having to tag along too, so she had brought her purse just in case.

Jamie was going to be a conjurer when he grew up, a fact he told everyone. He'd even made a flowing black cloak to prove it. Natty was going to be a famous horse rider, but she didn't yet know how. Mum and Dad couldn't even afford riding lessons, so owning her own pony was an impossibility. Would finding a four-leaved clover make any difference? She wondered. Mum put an arm around her shoulders and gave her a squeeze.

"Cheer up, Natty."

Natty managed a smile just as Penelope Potter cycled past on her gleaming new bicycle.

"Not going riding today, Penelope?" Mum asked.

"I am later," Penelope said. "When I've finished riding my bike."

A new bike *and* a pony, thought Natty. It's people like Penelope who have all the luck. And she trailed after her mum and brother to the bus-stop.

It was market day in town and they had to weave their way between the busy stalls to Cosby's

Magic Emporium, Jamie's favourite shop. It was tucked down a little side street off the market square. The shop front was faded and the paint peeled.

By the time Mum and Natty arrived, Jamie had disappeared inside.

Natty peered through the dingy window and was about to follow Mum in, when something at the back of the display caught her eye.

16

"Coming Natty?" Mum asked.

"Can I look a minute?"

"If you like. I'll see what Jamie's up to."

Tucked behind the card tricks, spectacles with funny noses, itching powder, pretend blood, extraordinary hats and magic rope was a poster. A chestnut pony with a white star and blaze, wearing the cheekiest expression, looked Natty straight in the eye. Natty couldn't imagine what a pony poster was doing amongst all the jokes and magic tricks but it made no difference. She wanted that poster. She knew the exact place she would pin it on her bedroom wall and, with a little laugh, hurried into the shop to ask how much it cost.

Chapter 2
The Poster

The shop bell tinkled and Natty
closed the door behind her. She
stepped round two large cardboard
boxes to where she could see Mum
and Jamie watching an old man
with gold-rimmed spectacles and
wispy grey hair demonstrate a
magic trick.

"Hocus pocus rim tin tiddle," he said and triumphantly held up what looked like an ordinary piece of rope.

Jamie gasped in admiration.

"That's brilliant! I saw you cut it up. I know I did." He took the offered rope and looked at it carefully. "I'll definitely take that trick."

The old man's eyes twinkled behind his spectacles.

"Thought you'd like that one."

"Natty, come and say hello to Mr Cosby." Mum waved at her to come forward.

"Interested in magic tricks are you, young lady?" the old man asked.

"Sort of," said Natty, not wanting to offend. "But I like ponies best. How much is the pony poster in the window, please?" Natty reached into her pocket for her purse.

"That pony needs a good home," said Mr Cosby, coming round from behind the counter. He shuffled past the cardboard boxes and opened what looked like a cupboard. When Mr Cosby took out the poster, Natty realized it was the door to the window display. "Four pounds."

"Four pounds!" Natty felt her hopes fade. She knew she didn't have four pounds.

Mum sighed. "Natty, are you sure you want another pony poster? It's a lot of money."

"Yes, I do. It's the most perfect picture. And if it was on my wall I could pretend it was my pony. We could have pretends together." She blushed. She didn't like talking about her pretends. Really they were a secret. She hurried to count out her money.

Mr Cosby closed the door to the cupboard that wasn't a cupboard and looked at the poster with satisfaction.

"This is the only one there is. There's not another like it." He walked back towards the counter and Natty was sure he whispered, "So you're very lucky to get it."

"Lucky?" said Natty. "Oh, yes, I am. The pony's so beautiful. I couldn't bear not to have him."

"Well, how much money have you got?" Mum asked.

"Three pounds twenty-seven pence," Natty replied, making a pile on the counter.

Jamie, who had been trying to work out the rope trick, suddenly took an interest.

"I've never seen horse posters here before."

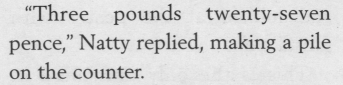

"Don't usually get them," agreed Mr Cosby. "This is a one-off special just waiting for your sister."

"So how did you know we were coming?"

Mr Cosby smiled in a vague sort of way and, realizing he was not going to get a reply, Jamie went back to his rope trick.

"Mum, please can you lend me seventy-three pence?" Natty asked.

"Are you sure, Natty? It's all your pocket money gone in one go."

"Quite sure," said Natty, who would have paid even more if necessary.

"He's called Ned," said Mr Cosby. "I think you'll find him good value for money. In fact I know you will."

Natty put her three pounds twenty-seven in Mr Cosby's hand and Mum added seventy-three pence. Smiling up at Mr Cosby, Natty was sure he gave her a

wink before rolling Ned into a
tube and slipping on an elastic
band.

"You look after him," he said,
handing Ned over. "Find him a nice
place on your wall and he'll look
after you. He's all yours now."

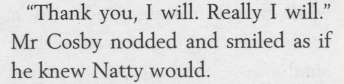

"Thank you, I will. Really I will."
Mr Cosby nodded and smiled as if
he knew Natty would.

On the bus going back Jamie
was impatient to get home, eager
to try out his new tricks. Natty
nursed her poster, thinking of
wonderful new pretends to have
with Ned. She was longing to take
another look at him.

When the bus drew into their
stop, Natty and Jamie jumped into
the lane leaving Mum to follow
more slowly.

"If you're going to run on ahead,"
she said to Jamie, "take the key." And
she handed it over.

Natty didn't run but did trotting
steps, pretending to be on Ned's
back.

When she got to the field gate, Penelope cantered past on Pebbles, turning him to jump a line of blue barrels. Natty would have stayed to watch, but the poster seemed to wriggle in her hand and remind her it was there. She didn't wait for Pebbles to jump the barrels again. She ran up the path to the front door and hurried in after Jamie. There was something important she had to do.

Chapter 3

The Pile on the Landing

Natty's feet clattered up the stairs and along the landing to her bedroom. It was the smallest room in the house – apart from the bathroom – and a bed, a chest of drawers, bookshelves and a desk were all that could be fitted in. Her hanging-up clothes went in the big wardrobe in Mum and Dad's bedroom. Sometimes, she minded that Jamie's room was twice the size, but he was the eldest and that was that. But she liked the view from her window, which included the whole of Pebbles's field and, from her bed, she was close enough to see Esmerelda, Prince and Percy, her three china ponies on the window-sill and all her pony pictures on the wall.

Natty slipped off the rubber band and her new poster unrolled. Ned looked up at her from the duvet while she reached for her paper pins, hardly taking her eyes off Ned's chestnut face. Somehow he seemed bigger, more head and shoulders than she remembered him in Mr Cosby's shop.

There, she was sure, she had seen his back and the top of his tail. Now he was like a pony looking out over his stable door. Puzzled, she thought she must have remembered wrong.

But it didn't stop her wanting his head to pop out of the picture. Of course, it didn't – which was sad.

She pinned Ned up above the chest of drawers, the best place for Natty to see him without getting a crick in her neck.

Then she flung herself on to her bed to try it out and glimpsed the four-leaved clover, still taped to the wall above her head.

"You did bring me luck," she told it. "You brought me Ned." She lay back and gave the chestnut pony a good long look.

Slowly she closed her eyes and began a new pretend. She told it in her head and it went like this.

– *Me and Penelope Potter are best friends. Not true in real life, but never mind! I collect a head collar from Penelope's tack room and Penelope is there. Penelope says, "Hello, Natty. Shall we go riding together?"*

I say, "Yes, that would be nice. I was just on my way to the field to bring Ned in."

Penelope says, "I'll come with you and fetch Pebbles."

Together we walk to the field gate and call.

"Ned!"

"Pebbles!"

The two ponies come trotting over.

One is a pretty chestnut with long flowing mane, one white stocking and a white star and blaze on his face...

Natty opened her eyes just to check on the star and blaze.

Yes, Ned was looking straight at her. She had got it right. The white stocking she had made up, not being able to see his feet. She closed her eyes again.

— *The other pony is a pretty dappled grey. In no time at all we fasten on the head collars and lead our ponies to their stables. I enjoy doing this because I am able to feed Ned juicy pieces of carrot and he nuzzles my pocket for more.*

Natty sighed. What would they do next? Oh, yes, grooming.

— *I am carefully bolting Ned's stable door when a voice calls me—*

"Natty. Natty, come down at once. It's teatime. I'm not telling you again." It was Mum's cross voice getting in the way and not the nice pretend voice she had given Penelope. Natty screwed up her eyes but otherwise didn't move. She wanted to brush Ned's ginger coat and make it gleam. This was her first real pretend with him and she didn't want to stop.

"Natty!" Jamie banged on her door.

"What?"

"It's teatime. Mum says you got to come now."

"I will come."

"And if you don't I've got to make you."

"Go away, horrid boy. I'm coming."
Natty sat up with a groan.

It wasn't fair. Why did tea have to
get in the way? The pretend was

going so well. On the other hand, she was feeling rather hungry. She swung her legs to the floor. Ned's eyes seemed to follow her to the door, which she liked.

"See you later," she whispered.

Downstairs in the living room the table had already been set. That was her and Jamie's job and she guessed Mum must have been calling for ages, got fed up and done it herself.

Dad wasn't back yet but Natty knew he would be soon. No wonder Mum was cross.

A key turned in the front door lock and the door slammed. It was Dad, and he came in looking really fed up.

"It's been one of those days," he said, slumping into a chair just as Mum came out from the kitchen.

"As bad as that, love?" she said, dropping a kiss on his forehead.

"I'll make you a nice cup of tea. Food'll be on the table in a couple of ticks."

They were just getting to the interesting bit of their meal, the cake course, when there was a startling crash, bang and gerflumph from upstairs. Natty froze, cake halfway to her mouth, and listened.

If she hadn't known it was
impossible she would have thought
a large animal was clomping
above their heads – like a cow or
a horse. A horse!

She dropped the cake and made
a dash for the door before anyone
else even moved. Racing upstairs
to her bedroom she found her
duvet crumpled and all the books
knocked on to it from the bottom
shelf. And something else was
wrong too. It took her a moment
or two to work out what it
was. Ned had disappeared. The
poster was still there but, apart

from a mass of blue sky, it was empty.

She stared astonished, until the rest of the family, pounding up the stairs, sent her running. The door into Mum and Dad's room was open and she peeped around it. Their bedspread was horribly crumpled too, although nothing else seemed different.

Then Natty noticed the funny smell. Everyone arrived at where it came from at the same time. Natty could hardly believe her eyes, for outside Jamie's room was a large pile of dung.

"Good grief," said
Dad. "Horse muck!"

Mum put her hands to her face.
"All over the carpet!" she wailed.

There was a moment's stunned silence, broken by something clumping in Jamie's room. Natty put her head round the door. A real live chestnut pony with one white stocking pawed at the carpet and swished his tail.

Natty gasped, eyes as round as pools. It was Ned.

"How did you get out of the picture?"

"I fell out. A mistake. I meant to jump." And he spoke!

Dad pushed the door open and in a blink Ned was gone. Natty couldn't work out where, until she saw a tiny pony trot along the window-sill and hide behind the curtain.

Her brain worked fast. She saw that Jamie's black cloak had been trodden on and was ripped. What with that and the dung on the landing no one was going to be pleased that there was a pony loose in the house, especially one that went from big to small, and seemed to come out of a picture.

"Is this some kind of a joke, Natty?" Dad asked.

"No," said Natty. "No." She couldn't think how to explain the smelly pile on the landing. "But dung is very good for roses."

Mum was stony-faced.

"I don't know how that mess got here but I want it cleaned up at once, Natty. Do you understand?" For some reason everyone was blaming her.

"Yes," said Natty. "I'll do it straight away." For although no one knew it was Natty's poster pony, Natty didn't want them to find out if she could possibly help it.

This, she realized, was a dream come true and she just wanted everyone to go away so she could find out more about it.

Chapter 4

The Tussle on the Carpet

Natty hurried to the garden. She took the shovel from the coal bunker and the bucket from the greenhouse. Mum, Dad and Jamie had gone back to finish their tea which, under the circumstances, Natty found surprising. She knew it wasn't her who had dumped horse pooh on the landing and couldn't imagine why they all thought it was. In the end she decided it was lucky that they did, even though she had been told to go to her room after clearing up and was definitely in disgrace.

She shovelled the smelly pile into the bucket, and carried it downstairs and out through the back door. Unsure where to put it, she took it to the bottom of the garden and dumped it on the compost heap. She washed the shovel and swilled the bucket and put them away where she found them.

Back on the landing, she sniffed the carpet and squirted it with carpet cleaner. She scrubbed hard and, by the time she'd finished, the messed-up patch was as good as new and much cleaner than the rest of the carpet.

She nipped into her bedroom to check Ned's picture. Still empty!

Then remembering the rip in Jamie's black cloak and Mum and Dad's crumpled bedspread she hurried to sort things out. Her own room could wait until later.

It didn't take a moment to straighten the bedspread, but the ripped cloak would take some time to mend. Thank goodness she did sewing with Mrs Plumley from next door, so she knew what to do. She didn't have much time. Soon Jamie would finish tea and, almost certainly, come upstairs to practise his magic tricks. She tiptoed across to the window-sill, expecting to find the miniature Ned behind the curtain. But he wasn't there. No time to look for him now.

She hurried into Mum and Dad's room in search of some black cotton, pins and a needle. She found the workbox in the big wardrobe. As quickly as she could, Natty pinned the torn sides together and began to sew.

She was not quick enough. She was only halfway down the rip when there was an angry cry from Jamie's bedroom. Now he'd discovered his cloak was missing, what was she going to do? Own up, she supposed.

"What do you mean you ripped it?"

"I didn't exactly say I ripped it. I said it got ripped. It was an accident and I am sewing it up."

"You'd better had. You wouldn't like it if I ripped something of yours, like that soppy pony poster."

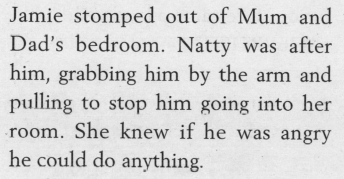

Jamie stomped out of Mum and Dad's bedroom. Natty was after him, grabbing him by the arm and pulling to stop him going into her room. She knew if he was angry he could do anything.

"Please," she wailed. "Please. I am mending it. I'm really sorry your cloak got ripped." She clung on, almost pulling off Jamie's sweatshirt while he kicked her bedroom door. Bang, bang, bang! She would not let him get to her poster. It would ruin everything. Jamie tried his hardest to shake her off. Then he took a deep breath and from his red and

furious face came a loud yell.
"GERROFF!"

But Natty had no intention of gerroffing. She had got a grip and wasn't letting go. It took all her strength, every bit, and she just hoped that someone, Mum or Dad, would arrive before Jamie finally won, because he was bigger and stronger, and would win in the end. She gritted her teeth as Jamie pulled her across the carpet and pushed at her bedroom door. It started to open.

From out of the corner of her eye she saw something small and chestnut, with a flowing mane and tail, canter through the crack into her bedroom.

There was a shrill whinny and the door banged shut, pushing Jamie back so hard that he knocked Natty into a crumpled heap. Before she could get up, Jamie shoved all his weight against the door and Natty thought he had won. But the door wouldn't budge.

To save face, Jamie jutted his chin forward and leaned towards her.

"If my cloak isn't mended properly, now, this instant, I'll get that poster and rip it into a million pieces, you see if I don't."

"I am mending your cloak. You know I am and I'll finish it now. I promise."

"You'd better had." At last Jamie's temper was cooling and, feeling safer now her bedroom door was stuck, Natty hurried to finish the sewing.

"If you two don't pack it in I'm coming up to knock your heads together!" Dad shouted up the stairs.

But as they had already packed it in Natty hoped he wouldn't bother. She went back into Mum and Dad's room and sat on the bed, feeling trembly. She and Jamie didn't often have fights but when they did, it was always horrid.

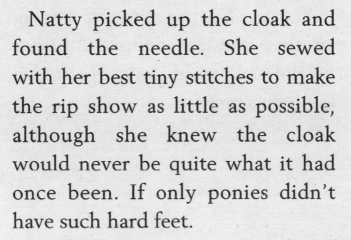

Natty picked up the cloak and found the needle. She sewed with her best tiny stitches to make the rip show as little as possible, although she knew the cloak would never be quite what it had once been. If only ponies didn't have such hard feet.

And as soon as she thought of ponies her mind began to spin. How could a pony come out of a picture, grow to its proper size, and in the blink of an eye shrink to almost nothing? How could it speak?

It was almost too much to take in.

And as Natty's fingers sewed, another question popped into her head. How would she get back into her bedroom?

Chapter 5
The Pony under the Bed

The cloak was finished at last, and when Natty held it up the mend was hardly visible. Mrs Plumley would have been proud of her and even Jamie was impressed when she gave it back, although he tried not to show it.

"Mmm, not bad," he said, putting it on with a flourish which turned the cloak into great bats' wings. "Want to see a trick?"

"Not just now," said Natty. "I've got things to do."

"Like unjamming your bedroom door?"

"Oh, it's not jammed now," said Natty, crossing her fingers and hoping she was right. "Something got wedged under it."

She hurried out of Jamie's room before he decided to come and look. Outside her door she put her ear to the wood and listened.

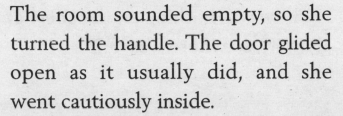

The room sounded empty, so she turned the handle. The door glided open as it usually did, and she went cautiously inside.

Ned's pony poster was still a blank and there was nothing on the bed except the books knocked from the shelf. She quickly put them back. She searched on her window-sill where Esmerelda, Prince and Percy stood in an undisturbed line, still looking across the front garden to Pebbles's field.

There was nothing on the chest of drawers, so where was he?

"Ned," she whispered. "Ned, where are you?" She got down on her hands and knees. Under the chest of drawers there was nothing but fluff.

She turned to the bed, lifting the duvet so she could get a proper look underneath it. "Ned, are you there?"

On the far side of the gloomy space she saw him trot in a circle and shake his head, then stop to paw the carpet before cantering towards her. He was the same size as Percy, the smallest of her china ponies. It was like having Percy come to life.

Natty kept quite still, her eyes
gleaming as if she couldn't quite
believe what she was seeing. When
Ned reached her knee, he jumped
and landed on her thigh. Before
Natty realized what she was doing,
she stroked his tiny back. There
was a sharp blast of air and she
was suddenly squashed against the
bed with Ned towering above her,
the size of Pebbles.

Ned was tacked up and ready with a saddle and bridle. It was astonishing.

"Get on," he said. "Quickly, before someone comes in."

Natty didn't need telling twice. She wriggled on to the bed, grabbed a handful of mane, and put a foot in the stirrup. The moment she was on his back a great wind blew. She shut her eyes against it.

When she opened them again she was clinging on like anything and Ned was cantering across a stretch of brown hillocks. He turned sharply around a large square tree and she nearly fell off. It took her a moment or two to realize that it wasn't a square tree but her bed leg, and that now she too had become tiny. She was wearing a hard hat and put a hand up to its silky smooth velvet, but not just that, she had on jodhpur boots, jacket, shirt and tie.

"I'm wearing riding things," she gasped, and couldn't imagine where her ordinary clothes had got to.

"Of course," said Ned. "Anyone ever teach you to ride?"

"Not really," said Natty. "When Penelope lets me, I walk about on

Pebbles. I have trotted twice but I've never really ridden."

"As I'm your magic pony, I shall teach you. That's what I'm here for."

"Yes, please," said Natty.

"Then take hold of the reins."
Natty picked them up with one
hand and kept hold of the mane
with the other. Being small, she
realized, meant it would be easy to
learn to ride in her bedroom – there
was masses of space. But Ned had
other ideas, and trotted on to the
landing. At the top of the stairs
Natty gasped, for the drop looked
huge.

"By the way," Ned said. "Tell your brother to keep his hands off my picture."

"Oh, he was cross about his magician's cloak, that's all," said Natty. "Now I've mended it, I'm sure he won't think of that again."

"It was lucky I managed to wedge the door shut in time. If that picture gets ripped that's the end of me."

"Oh, no!" said Natty.

"Oh, yes! So not a word to anyone about where I come from."

"Not a word. I promise." Natty clung on while Ned pawed at the carpet.

"Hold tight and off we go."

It was a shock when he jumped on to the first stair. Natty only just recovered her balance when he jumped to the next. She knew there were fourteen stairs and clung on grimly.

To her amazement, she was still on his back when Ned jumped to the hall floor. He trotted towards the living room, not seeming to mind Natty bouncing about like a sack of potatoes. Stretching high above them was the door, solid and thick, and open just enough for them to get through.

Mum and Dad were watching the television news, two giants sitting in mountainous chairs in front of a flickering screen. Spread across the carpet was a foot so big that Natty couldn't see to the other side. It was joined to a trousered leg that reached up forever, or so it seemed.

"Fancy a canter across the carpet?" said Ned, setting off.

Knowing she was no bigger than a little mouse, Natty felt afraid. Then no sooner had she thought mouse than she thought cat.

"Tabitha!" From the kitchen came the bang bang of the cat flap. "Stop," said Natty. "There's Tabitha. . .!"

Before she could properly warn him, Ned took off, galloping across the carpet towards Dad's big foot. Instead of going round it, Ned jumped the foot in a great bound, landing with a thud that left Natty halfway up his neck.

The pony didn't stop but turned and raced to the kitchen, sliding to a standstill on the tiles.

In the middle of the floor, paw raised, for until that moment she had been washing it, sat Tabitha.

"I've been trying to tell you!" panted Natty, just about clinging on. "We've got a cat!"

Chapter 6
Cat Scare

Two green eyes gleamed and a fluffy tail twitched. Ned reared up and his front legs thrashed. Natty fell, the terrible wind a roar in her ears, and landed to her astonishment in the sink, her normal size again. Wedged in the washing-up bowl with her legs

in the air, she struggled to pull
herself out. There wasn't much
room; Ned filled the kitchen. His
tail swished, knocking cutlery from
the draining-board and spice jars
from the rack. He snorted at
Tabitha and ignored the chaos

of jars and cutlery smashing and crashing at his feet.

Such a shock turned Tabitha into a brush cat. Her coat stuck out in all directions. But not for long.

Dad burst into the kitchen. "What on earth's going on?"

Ned vanished and Natty felt for the give-away riding hat. That had gone too, and her ordinary clothes were back.

"For goodness' sake, Natty! Get out of the sink!"

"I can't."

 Natty scanned the floor for signs of Ned. So did Tabitha, who was beginning to get the hang of this creature who went from small to big and back again. She and Natty caught sight of Ned at the same time, as he cantered behind the vegetable rack and hid at the back of the rubbish bin. Tabitha pounced and batted behind the bin with her paw.

It was a relief to Natty to find Dad's strong arms at her shoulders, lifting her from the sink to the floor. She wriggled round Dad and grabbed Tabitha.

"Stop it, you," she said crossly, and unceremoniously dumped the struggling cat in the living room and shut the door.

Dad looked grimly at the mess of knives, forks and broken jars that scattered the floor.

"What is going on?"

"It was an accident," Natty said, feeling her wet bottom. "I'll clear it up."

"I should think you will," said Dad. "With the dustpan and brush. Mind you don't cut yourself on the glass."

"I'll get the dustpan." Before darting to the cupboard where the dustpan was kept, Natty opened the back door. She wanted Ned to escape to the garden and find a safer hiding place than behind the rubbish bin.

The moment Natty began to sweep, Mum opened the living-room door.

"Oh, what a mess!" she exclaimed.

And not being a cat to miss an opportunity, Tabitha raced for the rubbish bin. Natty dropped the dustpan and dived. The rubbish bin went flying and through the hail of empty baked beans tins, wrappers and cartons, a tiny pony bolted for the garden. Tabitha scrambled from between Natty's arms and gave chase.

"Leave that cat alone," scolded Dad, stopping Natty in her tracks. "You're just making everything worse."

"The kitchen's a pigsty," said Mum. "Natty, how could you?" Natty

didn't even try and explain. With
one eye on the back door she righted
the rubbish bin and swept as fast as
she could.

Ages later the kitchen was clean
again, and Natty hurried to put the
dustpan away. There was no sign of
Ned or Tabitha.

"Can I go now?" she asked.

"Yes," said Mum. "Straight up
to bed and get
those wet jeans
off."

"But—"

"You heard
what I said."

Natty knew there was no arguing, so after a quick peep out of the back door she hurried back through the living room and upstairs. Only instead of going to her bedroom, she went to the bathroom where she closed and locked the door.

The bathroom window opened out above the kitchen roof. Natty had never actually climbed out from here before, but Jamie had. Jamie had reached the ground that way. If he could do it, so could she.

Natty put down the toilet lid and climbed on to it. Then with a foot in the hand basin she balanced her knee on the window-sill and opened the window.

From there she scanned the garden for signs of Ned and Tabitha. Washing hung limp on the line and the shed door was open. She would have to be careful. The twitch of a tabby-cat tail drew her eye to the canopy of rhubarb leaves billowing out from the vegetable patch. Tabitha, it seemed, was underneath.

Natty pulled herself up and perched in the open window. Turning, she eased herself down, hooking her arms over the sill until her toes touched the tiles of the kitchen roof. She had made it.

Crouching low she decided the best way to the ground was by the old trellis nailed to the wall at the far end. She crawled along the tiles and let herself down carefully.

Hoping she could not be seen from the living room, she hurried down the path, ducked under the washing, and crouched to peer under the rhubarb. It was a dark, dense, stalk-filled forest. Ned, if he was there, could be hiding anywhere. Tabitha's green eyes glinted.

"You leave Ned alone, Tabby," she

warned. "He's a pony, not a mouse."
Tabitha blinked but her tail
twitched just the same. "Ned, are
you there?"

There was a thump and a clump
and a bang.

"I'm here." The voice didn't come

from under the rhubarb, it came from the shed, where Ned's head peeped out, proper pony size, just as if he was looking out from a stable.

"What are you doing in there?" Natty asked.

"Hiding, of course. What do you think?"

Natty ran to the shed and put her arms round Ned's neck. She was so pleased he was safe! Then she noticed the saddle and bridle had gone. She looked around for them. On the floor lay Dad's claw hammer and wooden mallet.

"Sorry, I knocked the tools off with my bottom," said Ned. Natty picked them up and put them on the workbench.

"But where's the saddle and bridle?"

"They come and go when I don't need them," said Ned. "Just like your riding things."

"So it's real magic then," said Natty, eyes wide.

"Hat, boots, jacket, saddle, bridle, it's all real magic, including me!" Ned gave her an affectionate push with his nose.

"And now you've found me you can help me get back to my picture.

That's enough excitement for one day. Ready to carry me?"

"But I can't!"

"Yes, you can." And, in the blink of an eye, Ned was his tiny self, trotting across the floor.

Natty scooped him up in cupped hands and, with a quick look to check no one was watching, hurried to the trellis.

She balanced Ned on her shoulder and slowly climbed, one foot then the next, arms pulling until they reached the roof. Here Ned jumped, landing neatly in the gutter. He trotted along the black gully, leaping the leaves and twigs that had collected there.

Natty crawled beside him across the tiles. She was beginning to think they would make it without further mishap, until she looked up and saw Tabitha crouched on the window-sill. Ned scrambled from the gutter and Tabitha flew at him, claws unsheathed. In a trice Ned was big again, balancing dangerously on the slippery tiles. With a terrific effort he leaned back on his hocks and jumped for the bathroom window.

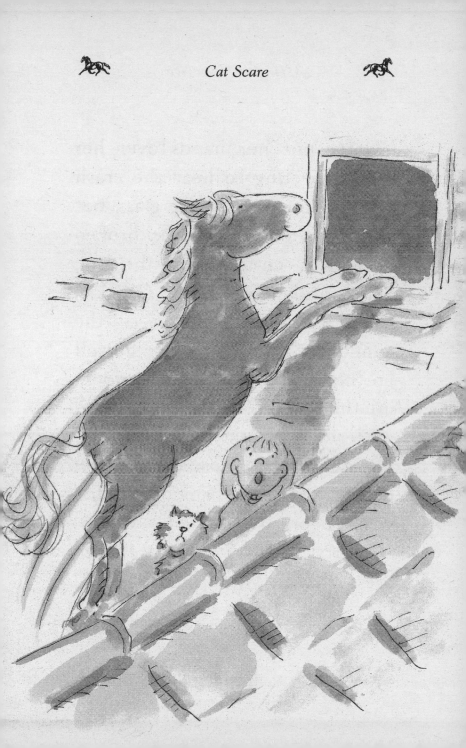

Natty put her hands over her ears, expecting to hear the crash and splinter of breaking glass, but there was only a silence, broken by Tabitha scuttling from the roof, her confidence shaken. Quickly, Natty put her hands over the window-sill and hauled herself up. She tumbled into the bathroom in time to see the tiny Ned cantering across the bathmat. She managed to close the window before an angry banging started on the door.

"Hurry up, Natty. You've been ages. What are you doing in there?"

It was Jamie, fed up with waiting. "Coming," said Natty, undoing the lock. But before she had a chance to pick Ned up, the door was pushed open and Jamie barged in.

"You're not the only one who wants to get ready for bed." Ned shied sideways and galloped for the landing.

"Sorry," said Natty and rushed after him.

"So I should think." And the bathroom door slammed without Jamie noticing a thing.

Inside her bedroom, Natty closed the door and ducked down to look for Ned under the bed. He wasn't there. Neither was he on the window-sill or under the chest of drawers. It was only when she sat on her bed that she saw he was back in the poster. She sighed a huge sigh of relief.

But a picture pony cannot talk, and as Natty pulled off her wet jeans and pulled on her dry pyjama bottoms she began to miss him.

"Ned? Did you really happen?" she asked, running a finger across the poster's shiny surface. It was cool and only paper, not a bit like the warm silky fur she longed to feel.

She sat back on the bed and stared up at him.

"We had an adventure, didn't we?" she said at last. "A scary one." But already she wasn't quite sure. It could have been a pretend, except she'd never have thought up such an exciting one.

Mum came in to kiss her goodnight.

"Night night, love," she said, stroking Natty's hair. "Lost in a dream as usual."

"Not really." Natty smiled. "At least, I don't think so."

"Well if you aren't, you soon will be. Have sweet ones," said Mum. "See you in the morning."

It was after Mum closed the door that Natty noticed a long chestnut hair on her duvet. She picked it up and her heart beat fast with excitement. It must have come from Ned's tail.

"It is true," she said. "You did happen." Natty looped the hair carefully over her four-leaved clover so that it hung above her on the wall. Then she snuggled down.

Maybe, just maybe, Ned would come to life again soon and, with that wish on her lips and her fingers crossed to make it come true, she fell fast asleep.

The End

Meet Airy Fairy.

Her wand is all wonky, her wings
are covered in sticking plaster
and her spells are always a muddle!
But she's the cutest fairy around!

Margaret Ryan

Airy Fairy

Magic Mischief!

How can one little
fairy get into such
BIG trouble?

SCHOLASTIC

Margaret Ryan

Airy Fairy

Magic Muddle!

How can one little fairy get into such BIG trouble?

■ SCHOLASTIC

Margaret Ryan

Airy Fairy

Magic Mess!

How can one little
fairy get into such
BIG trouble?

SCHOLASTIC